NORA

The girl who ate and ate and ate ...

Andrew Weale & Ben Cort

Andersen Press

The only thing that I can say
Of Nora Fatima Buffet,
Is that she was a greedy-guts,
Who loved to eat all kinds of nuts,

And buns, and ice cream, runny cheese,
Pork sausages, chocolate fudge cake, peas,
Smoked mackerel, fried eggs, vindaloo,
Rice pudding, streaky bacon, stew.

THIS BOOK BELONGS TO:

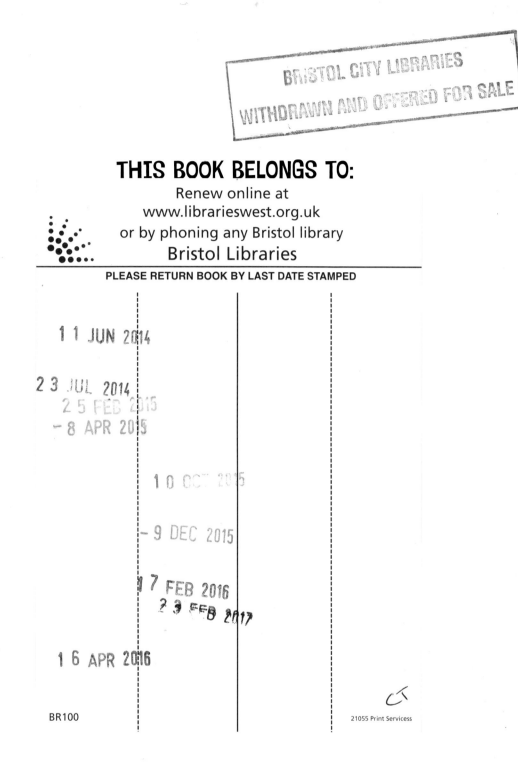

To Eva, who hasn't landed on the moon . . . yet! A.W.

For Mum with all my love. B.C.

This paperback edition first published in 2012 by Andersen Press Ltd.,

20 Vauxhall Bridge Road, London SW1V 2SA.

Published in Australia by Random House Australia Pty.,

Level 3, 100 Pacific Highway, North Sydney, NSW 2060.

First published in Great Britain in 2011 by Andersen Press Ltd.

Text copyright © Andrew Weale, 2011.

Illustration copyright © Ben Cort, 2011.

The rights of Andrew Weale and Ben Cort to be

identified as the author and illustrator of this work

have been asserted by them in accordance with the

Copyright, Designs and Patents Act, 1988.

All rights reserved.

Colour separated in Switzerland by Photolitho AG, Zürich.

Printed and bound in China by C&C Offset Printing CO. LTD;

10   9   8   7   6   5   4   3

British Library Cataloguing in Publication Data available.

ISBN 978 1 84939 382 9

This book has been printed on acid-free paper

And all these yummy things she ate
Heaped up together on one plate.
And then, of course, when she was through,
She licked the plate and ate that too!

One day her mum took hours to make
The hugest gooey chocolate cake,
But when her mother turned her back,
Dear Nora thought she'd have a snack.

Her mother sent her up to bed,
"You'll have no dinner now," she said.
Oh! Nora stormed up to her room,
She slammed the door and it went

BOOM!

But if you think that that was it,
You don't know her one tiny bit.
She opened up her secret drawer,
That burst with **sweets**
and **snacks**
and **more.**

But still she was not satisfied,
Until with greedy eyes she spied
Her wardrobe, desk, computer, chair,
A box of toys, her

teddy bear!

She piled them all onto her bed
And then, instead of using bread,
She curled the mattress round her things
And made a sandwich fit for kings.

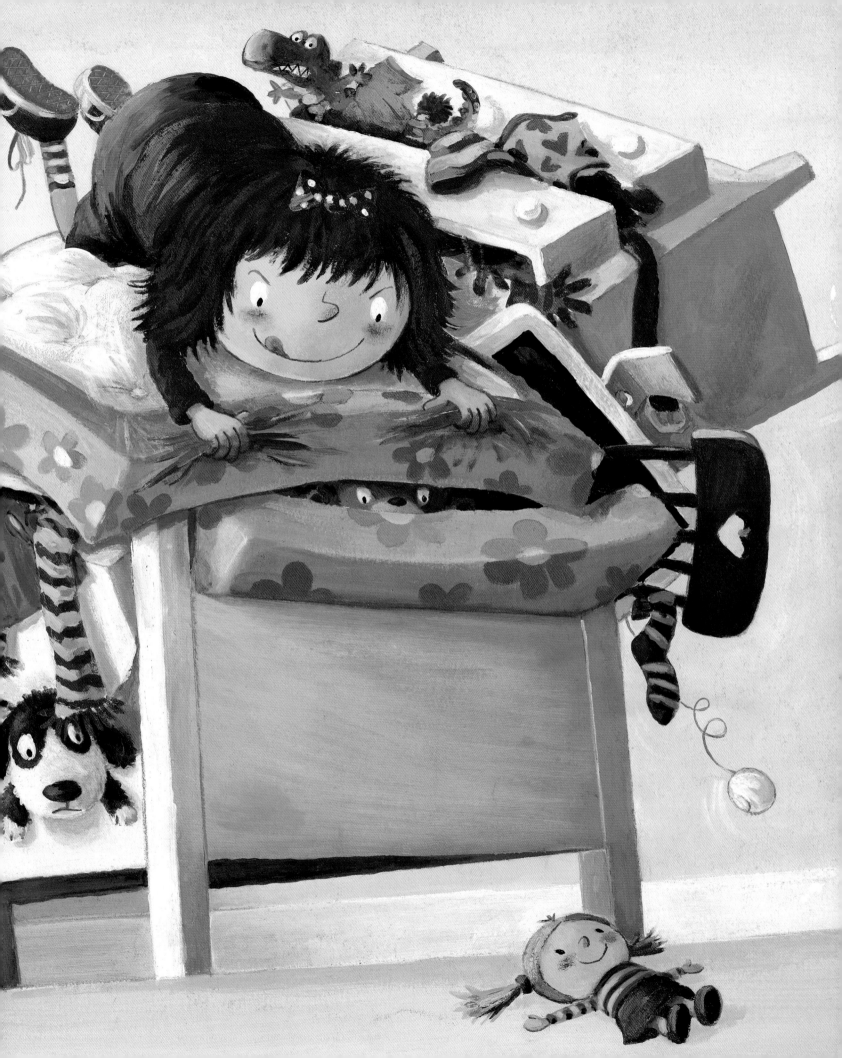

But even after all this stuff,
Dear Nora cried, "**It**'s **not enough!**"
Till she glanced down and with a grin
She saw what she was **standing in.**

Her shoes and socks, she didn't care,
She gobbled every single pair.
And when she'd finished off her shirt,
She ate her jumper for dessert.

They all went down in one

huge

SLURP!

Then Nora did a great big . . .

Out flew all the things she'd **swallowed**,
And you'll **never guess** what **followed** . . .

Dear Nora whizzed like a balloon

Until she landed on the moon.

And on a starry night – I hope –
You'll see her with your telescope.
But don't feel sorry for her, please!
For what's the moon made out of . . .

... CHEESE!

OTHER BOOKS TO ENJOY:

9781849393843

9781849393874

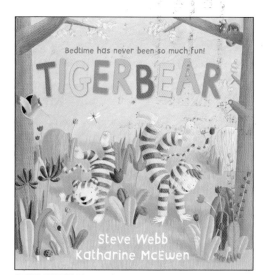

9781849392259

9781849393591

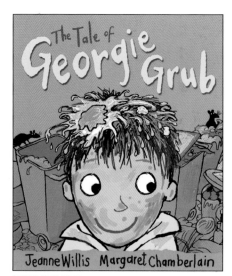

9781849390651

9781849392198